AUDREY WOOD **THE NAPPING HOUSE**

Illustrated by
DON WOOD

SCHOLASTIC INC.
New York Toronto London Auckland Sydney
Mexico City New Delhi Hong Kong

ISBN 0-590-97546-3

13   4/0

Printed in Mexico   49

First Scholastic printing, September 1996

The original paintings were done in oil on pressed board.
The text is Clearface Roman, set by Thompson Type, San Diego, California.
The display type is Clearface Bold, set by Thompson Type, San Diego, California.
Separations were made by Heinz Weber, Inc., Los Angeles, California.
Designed by Dalia Hartman

For Maegerine Thompson Brewer

There is a house,
a napping house,
where everyone is sleeping.

And in that house
there is a bed,
a cozy bed
in a napping house,
where everyone is sleeping.

And on that bed
there is a granny,
a snoring granny
on a cozy bed
in a napping house,
where everyone is sleeping.

And on that granny
there is a child,
a dreaming child
on a snoring granny
on a cozy bed
in a napping house,
where everyone is sleeping.

And on that child
there is a dog,
a dozing dog
on a dreaming child
on a snoring granny
on a cozy bed
in a napping house,
where everyone is sleeping.

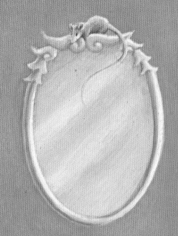

And on that dog
there is a cat,
a snoozing cat
on a dozing dog
on a dreaming child
on a snoring granny
on a cozy bed
in a napping house,
where everyone is sleeping.

And on that cat
there is a mouse,
a slumbering mouse
on a snoozing cat
on a dozing dog
on a dreaming child
on a snoring granny
on a cozy bed
in a napping house,
where everyone is sleeping.

And on that mouse
there is a flea. . . .

Can it be?
A wakeful flea
on a slumbering mouse
on a snoozing cat
on a dozing dog
on a dreaming child
on a snoring granny
on a cozy bed
in a napping house,
where everyone is sleeping.

A wakeful flea
who bites the mouse,

who scares the cat,

who claws the dog,

who thumps the child,

who bumps the granny,

who breaks the bed,

in the napping house,
where no one now is sleeping.